Elly's Adventure Saving the Coral

Written and Illustrated by
Linda Nissen Samuels

PATO PRESS

www.patopress.com

Pato Press
P O Box 70114
London
N12 2DT
Visit us on the World Wide Web at www.patopress.com

Story and illustrations by Linda Nissen Samuels

British Library Cataloguing-in-Publication Data
A catalogue record for this book is available from the British Library.

ISBN: 9780995479036

Typeset in Chewy Blossom and Chelsea Market Pro
Font Diner© – www.fontdiner.com
Book Design and Production
Clare O Hagan, Basil Samuels

The publisher's policy is to use paper manufactured
from sustainable forests.

To Benjamin, Jack, Ava and Leo

Elly went down to the seaside in a car. Lots of other cars were going too, and there was a big traffic jam.
The people were getting hot and bothered.

The cars were getting hot and bothered.

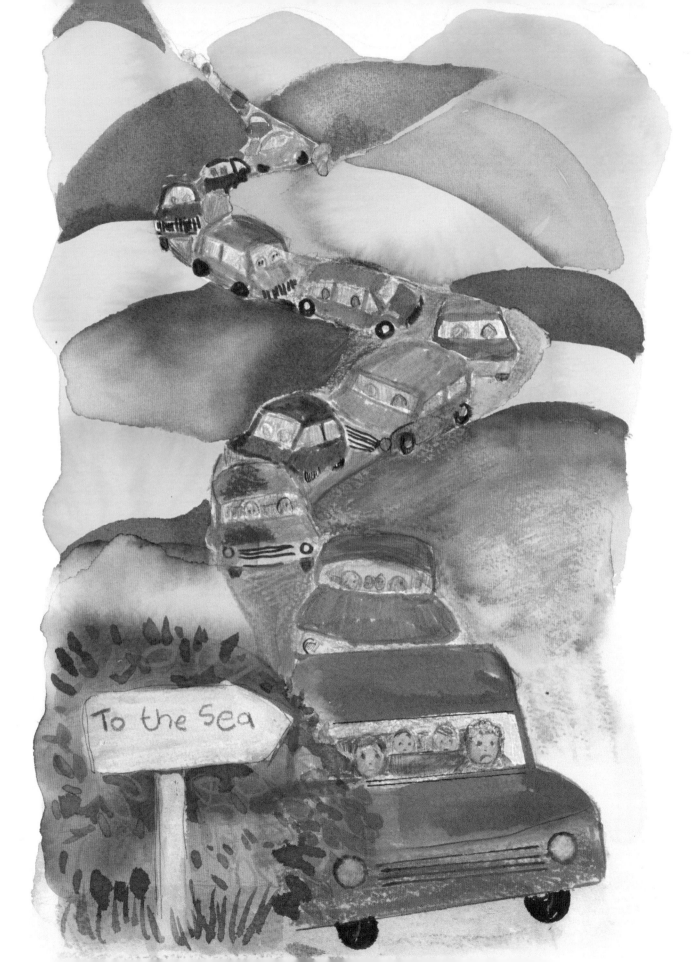

When at last they got there,
Elly couldn't wait to jump
in the sea and see the coral.
His brother Abi paddled on the edge.

When Elly reached the deep water, he dived down and there was the most amazing sight.
Beautiful fish and coral in every colour you could imagine! He swam back quickly to tell Abi about it.

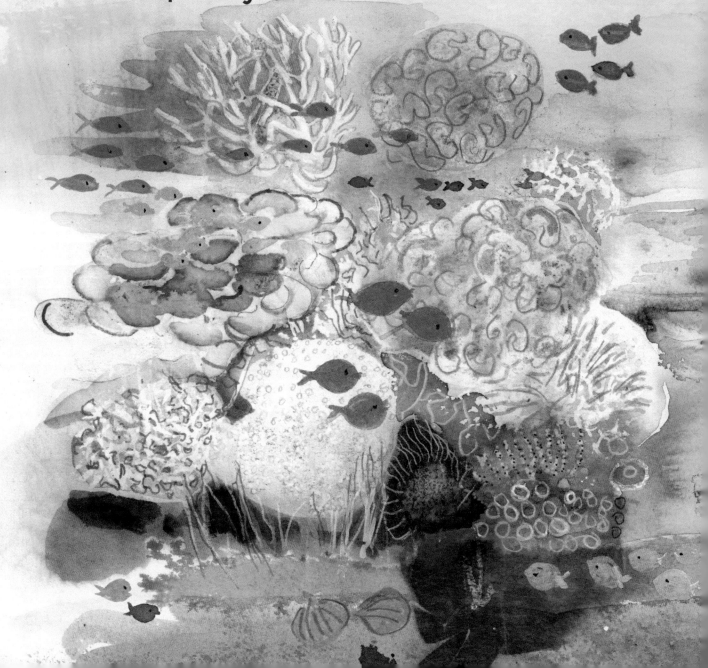

Just then, he saw his friend Leesha arriving on her bike.

"Come and see the beautiful coral!" he called.

"Not all of it is beautiful." she replied when she reached him.

"What do you mean?" Elly asked.

But Leesha just jumped into the water and beckoned Elly to follow her.

This time they swam further
out and round a big rock,
and Elly got a nasty surprise.

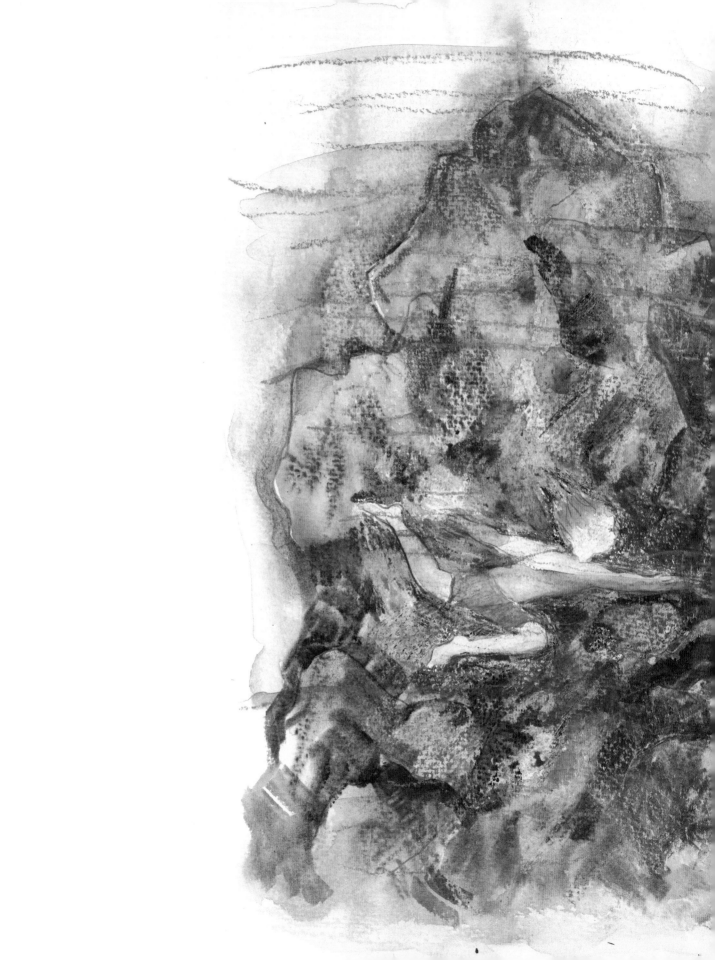

All the coral was bleached white
as far as the eye could see.
There wasn't a single bit of colour!

What has happened to the coral?"
Elly asked Leesha, as soon as they
got back to the shore.

"Well," said Leesha, "most people think
that coral is a plant, but actually it's
lots of tiny animals called polyps
living very close together."

"I never knew that!" said Elly.

"The polyps eat plants called algae
that grow in the sea,"
Leesha continued.
"But all the algae is dying because
the sea is getting too warm.
When there isn't enough algae,
the colourful coral turns white."

The three children started to walk down the beach.

"But why is the sea getting too warm?" Elly asked.

"It's we human beings' fault." Leesha explained. "We use our cars too much and waste electricity, and we don't recycle enough.

All of those things make the earth get too hot — and then the sea gets too hot as well."

That evening, Elly got out his paints and made a BIG flag. It said,

"Keep the planet cool.
Bring back the colour into coral!"

"Let's tell everyone to try to use cars and electricity less." he said.

"Yes!" said Leesha.
"And to recycle their rubbish instead of throwing it away."

The next day, lots of people came with Elly, Abi and Leesha to the beach and there wasn't a single car!

Can you see all the different ways of arriving? And... who do you think is going to get to the water first?

Now that you have read
Elly's Adventure Saving the Coral,

YOU can help Cool Planet Earth
like this:

Use cars less

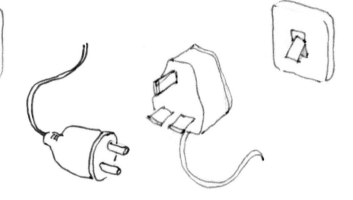

Switch off
electricity when
you don't need it

Recycle

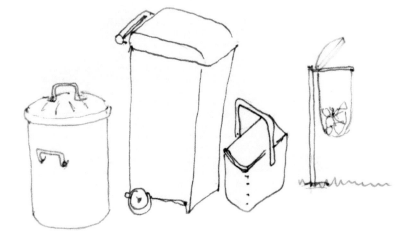

Now learn to draw an undersea scene with the step by step book – Draw Water and Other Things.

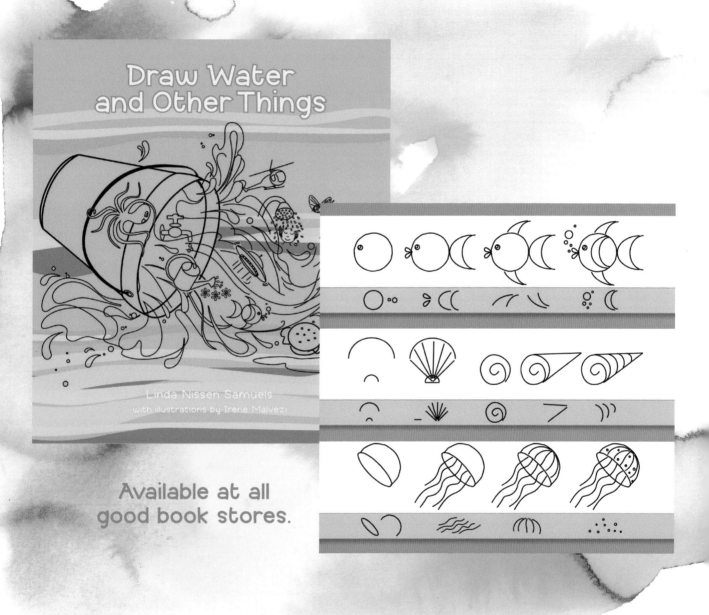

Draw Water and Other Things

Linda Nissen Samuels
with illustrations by Irene Malvezi

Available at all good book stores.

PATO PRESS

www.patopress.com

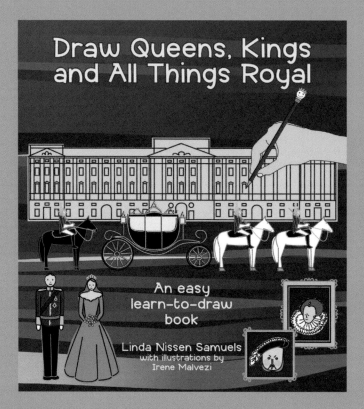

Learn to draw Buckingham Palace, Windsor Castle, Henry VIII, Elizabeth I, Charles II, Queen Victoria and many more in a few easy steps. This wonderful book is based on Linda Nissen Samuels innovative drawing method. From easy step-by-step drawings with simple lines and circles, learn how to recognise the underlying shapes of objects, and transfer this skill to more complicated shapes as your confidence increases.

Linda Nissen Samuels with illustrations by Irene Malvezi.

available from www.royalcollectionshop.co.uk

About the Author and Illustrator

Born in South Africa, Linda Nissen Samuels, grew up surrounded by the beauty of the natural world. As an artist, she reflects that vision on canvas. She is passionate about the preservation of the environment and the need to inspire children to appreciate and protect the balance of nature.

Linda's African landscape images, used by the charity WaterAid as their annual greeting cards, have proved extremely popular worldwide, raising substantial funds to support the provision of safe water. Her work has also been exhibited at the Royal Society of Marine Artists.

Linda has run her own gallery in London and mounted several one-woman exhibitions in France. She has been awarded eight medals, including five Golds, at the International Grand Prix of Art in Cannes.

In recent years, Linda has focused on creating books to make drawing accessible to everyone and range of beautifully illustrated children's books to introduce young readers to environmental issues.

Easy draw book 'Draw Water and Other Things' is now in its second edition, and has been described as a 'classic'. Its companion, 'Draw Queens, Kings and All Things Royal' was published in 2015 and is on sale at Buckingham Palace, London. Suitable for all ages, Linda's simple, easy to follow diagrams make these books a must for all aspiring artists, unsure how to begin putting pencil to paper.

In 'Elly's Adventure in the Animal Park', the first book in Elly's Ecology series, Linda's vibrant watercolour plates compliment her story in which Elly comes to realise how important insect life is to the survival of the planet.

The second book in the series 'Elly's Adventure Down by the Sea', is an enchanting story that teaches children about the importance of protecting the marine environment. Elly and his friends want to build a fantastic sandcastle on the beach – but is a plastic bottle and straw, what they should use to decorate it?

To find out more about Linda and her books visit:
www.patopress.com

Printed in Great Britain
by Amazon